My Favorite CHRISTMAS Stories

My Favorite CHRISTMAS Stories

tiger tales

Contents

The Magical SNOWman

by Catherine Walters

Illustrated by Alison Edgson

It was a clear, sparkling
winter's day. Little Rabbit had
been busy all morning, piling
snow to make a snowman.
"Good work, Little Rabbit,"
said Daddy. "Could you finish it
later, though? I need you to find
some berries for our breakfast."

"Snowman will be sad if I leave him now," Little Rabbit said.

"He'll be fine," said Daddy gently. "He's just a snowman. He isn't real."

"He *is* real!" said Little Rabbit. But Little Rabbit agreed to do as Daddy told him.

Daddy smiled as he gave Little Rabbit a kiss. "Don't go too far," he said.

"I won't!" said Little Rabbit.

"Mmm, one for the basket and one for me," he sang as he skipped down the path. Soon his paws were sticky with purple juice.

Little Rabbit was
having so much fun . . .

that he hardly noticed
the snow begin to fall.

A robin flitted
ahead of him and
he followed it . . .

dancing through the
drifting snowflakes
and bare trees.

Then the robin flew away. Little
Rabbit stopped and looked around.
He wasn't sure which way he had
come. The swirling snow made
everything look different.

"What will I do?" he cried.
"How will I get home?"

As if in answer, a soft light sparkled through the trees. Smiling through the falling snow was his very own Snowman!

"I *knew* you were real!" said Little
Rabbit. "But Snowman, I feel so alone."
"Not all alone," smiled Snowman.
"I was there, too, little friend. I am
always there for you."

Snowman dusted flakes
from Little Rabbit's fur
and lifted him onto his
shoulders.
"I'll take you home,"
he said. "Hold on
tight!"

They slid down the hill . . .
WHOOOOOOOOOSH!

and landed in a snowy heap
by a frozen stream. WHUMPH!

"Here we go!" Snowman laughed
as he held Little Rabbit's paw.
    The world whisked by in a
shimmer of silver frost. It felt as
if they were flying.
    "I'm coming home, Daddy!"
Little Rabbit called.

WHEEEEEEEEEEEE!

Suddenly, Snowman skidded to a halt at
the bottom of a hill.

"We'll have to walk now," he said, as he
swung Little Rabbit into his soft arms.

"Are we there yet?" yawned Little Rabbit.

"Not far now," said Snowman.

Meanwhile, Daddy Rabbit was hurrying
through the whirling snow. He was very
worried and he shivered in the icy wind.

"Little Rabbit!" he called. "Little Rabbit!
Where are you?"

"Daddy!" cried Little Rabbit when
he heard his call. He leaped from
Snowman's arms and bounded up
the yard.

Daddy Rabbit swept him up and hugged
him tight, forgetting all about the berries.
"Thank goodness you're safe!" he said.
"I was so worried about you, all alone."

"I wasn't alone," said Little Rabbit. "Snowman took care of me."

"Oh, did he now?" Daddy chuckled.

Snowman stood quietly in the winter darkness. Little Rabbit smiled at him. And he saw Snowman was smiling, too.

The First Snow

by M. Christina Butler

Illustrated by Frank Endersby

Little Deer peeked out of his bed and blinked
in the morning sunshine.

"Yikes!" he squeaked. "Where did everything go?"

Everything looked different. The woods were
covered with a huge white blanket.

Just then, Rabbit came skidding over, shouting, "Snow! Snow! Look at the snow!"
"Yippeee!" Squirrel cried, jumping out of a pine tree.

"What's happened?" squeaked Little Deer. "Where is all the grass?"

"It's under the snow," giggled Rabbit, beginning to dig. "Ta-daah!" he said as a tuft of icy grass appeared.

Little Deer nibbled a bit here and nibbled a bit there. The cold, crispy grass was very strange.

"Catch me if you can!" cried Rabbit, skipping off.

"Easy peasy," laughed Squirrel. "Come on, Little Deer!"

Little Deer stepped carefully into the cold, slippery snow . . . .

BUMP!

He slipped and slid and landed on his bottom! He tried to get up again and . . .

BUMP!
THUMP!

He fell on his nose in a snowdrift!

"Ow-ooh!" he cried.
"I HATE the snow!
I want to go home!"

"Don't go, Little Deer," said Rabbit.
"We're going to build a snowman!"
said Squirrel.
"And we can't do it without you,"
added Rabbit.

41

So Rabbit made a snowball
and they all began to push.

Slowly it got bigger and bigger . . .

and soon it was so big
they couldn't push it
any farther!

"Let's make the snowman a head!"
said Squirrel.

"He'll be bigger than me!" Little Deer
laughed.

But with a creak and a groan the
snowball began to roll down the hillside.

"Oh, no!" shouted Little Deer. "Stop
that snowman!"

Slipping and sliding, they all chased
down the hill. Faster and faster the
snowball rolled, and faster and faster
they tumbled after it . . . .

SWOOSH! They skimmed off the bottom of the hillside, spun across the ice, and landed, **CRASH!** in a big, snowy heap.

"That was awesome!" gasped Little Deer, as they all shook off the snow.

Slowly and slippily, wibbling and wobbling, they tried to stand up . . . BUMP!

SWOOSH!

THUMP!
They skidded and slipped, and down they fell again and again!

"Eeek!" squeaked Squirrel.
"Aaaah!" giggled Rabbit.

"Hooray!" shouted Little Deer, up on his feet at last. "Let's skate!"

On and on they twirled until the
moon shone bright, and stars twinkled
in the deep blue sky. Little Deer's first
snow had been such a surprise, but it
had been the best fun ever!

The Christmas Angels

by Claire Freedman   Illustrated by Gail Yerrill

Hush now, can you hear
the angels singing,
High up in the
frosty midnight air?
Voices ringing, singing
songs of Christmas,
Happiness for all
the world to share.

As we count the days
until it's Christmas,
Filling all our homes
with light and love,
Angels share these
special times of gladness,
Celebrating with us
high above.

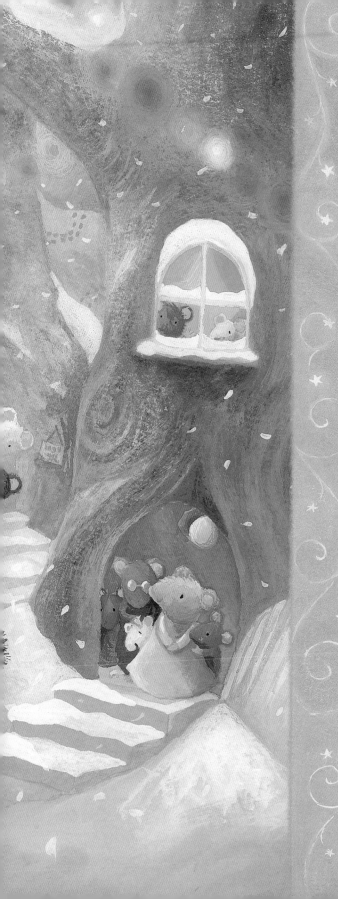

When we gather 'round
to sing sweet carols,
Each of us with
happy heart aglow,
In the sky, the angels
all sing with us,
As on that first
Christmas long ago.

When we help and care
for one another,
High above, the angels
see it, too.
Every little act of
love and kindness
makes the gentle angels
smile at you.

As dusk falls, the angels fly above us,
Lighting all the stars up in the sky.
When you see a silver star shine brightly,
Then you know an angel is nearby.

As the daylight fades
to gentle shadows,
And soft moonbeams
shimmer, silver-white,
Tender angels watch us
while we're sleeping,
Keeping us safe through
the moonlit night.

Hush now, can you hear the angels singing?
Sweetest songs of peace from heaven above,
Christmas songs of hope and joy and wonder,
Filling every happy heart with love.

A Long Way From Home

by Elizabeth Baguley · Illustrated by Jane Chapman

At bedtime in the burrow,
Noah was squished and squashed
by sleepy rabbits.
"Oh, no," he said. "Not again!
Move over, Ella."

Ella squeezed over, folding her
arms around Noah like he was
her teddy bear.
"Too hot!" muttered Noah.
"Too many rabbits!"
So out into the night he went.

"What are you doing out here, Smallest Bunny?"
asked Albatross, swooping down.

"There's no room," snuffled Noah. "And Ella
is always squashing me."

"But she's your favorite sister."

"It doesn't keep her from squashing me," said Noah.

To cheer him up, Albatross told Noah about the land of the North Star, where sky and snow went on forever.

"No rabbits there," said Noah, sighing. "I wish I could come with you to the frozen North."

"Hop on, then, Smallest Bunny," Albatross said.

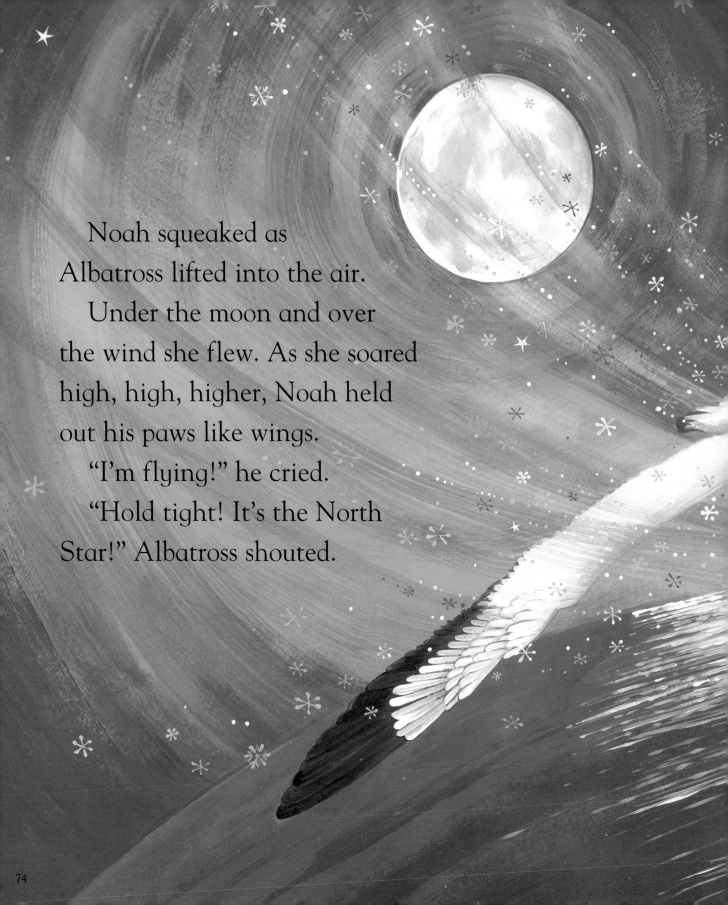

Noah squeaked as Albatross lifted into the air.

Under the moon and over the wind she flew. As she soared high, high, higher, Noah held out his paws like wings.

"I'm flying!" he cried.

"Hold tight! It's the North Star!" Albatross shouted.

From the North Star
came a wild tornado of
snow, and before Noah
knew it, he had toppled
into the storm!

Swept up by the wind,
he tumbled and rolled . . .

down . . .

and down . . .

to land—puff!—
in the snow.

Noah was all alone and for a moment he
was afraid, then he looked around at the empty
white space and hopped with excitement.
"No squish!" he cried. "No squash!"
Noah danced in the snow.

He skated and slid and threw snowballs. But then—whoosh!—he slipped into a hole and down an ice slide, going faster and faster until . . .

. . . Noah skidded to a stop.
Oh, no! Rabbits everywhere!
    As Noah opened his mouth to
complain, the other rabbits did,
too. But the only sound was
Noah's tiny squeak.

"Mirror rabbits!" he gasped at his
reflections in the ice.

Noah was in an ice cave, an ice hall,
an ice palace! It was as big as Big and
as quiet as Quiet.

And there was no one there but him.

Noah made a cool, roomy snow-nest.
"At last, no nest-sharings!" he pronounced
and lay royally down to sleep.

When Noah woke, his fluff
was frozen and he was cold to
the bone.

Shivering in his lonely bed,
he thought about his snuggly sister
Ella, squeezed into their nest with
all the cozy night-snufflings of his
family.

Even Noah's tears froze. How he
longed to go home!

So out of the palace he fled,
slipping and scrambling up the
ice slide until he came out under
the open sky where the stony
moon shone.

"Albatross!" shouted Noah. "Where
are you?"

There was no answer, only the
empty creaking of the ice.

But then Noah heard a feathery whisper on the wind. He looked up and saw wide wings. It was Albatross!

"Smallest Bunny!" she said, relieved. "I've been looking for you everywhere!"

She swung Noah on to her back and gratefully he nestled into her warm down, thinking only of home.

Back in the nest, Ella rolled over.
Noah was wonderfully squished and
squashed. He was delightfully crumpled and
crammed. He was Ella's teddy bear again.
Noah snuggled into her fluff and with
a sigh, he fell happily asleep.

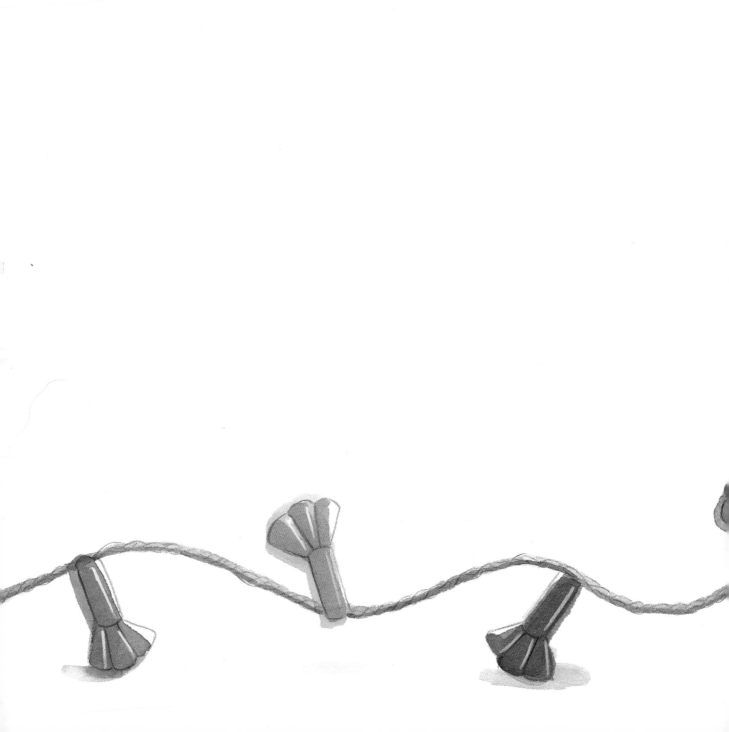

The Best
Christmas
Ever!

by Marni McGee
Illustrated by Gavin Scott

Milly Mouse was **so excited!**
Christmas was only one day away,
and the little mouse could
hardly wait.

She had swept and scrubbed until everything sparkled. She had fluffed and dusted until she sneezed.

ACHOO!

Milly gathered apples and nuts from the cellar.

BIG NUTS

BIGGER NUTS

EVEN BIGGER NUTS

Flour

In a flurry of flour, she baked an apple-nut pie.

She poured honey and spices into a kettle.
Standing on tiptoe, she sniffed—and smiled.
"Christmas just **wouldn't** be Christmas," she said,
"without my hot honey punch and apple-nut pie."

Milly bundled up, then
scampered out into the snow.
Her black boots crunched as she
walked here and there, gathering
all the ivy she could carry.

"Christmas just **wouldn't** be Christmas," she puffed, "**without** fresh ivy for my wreath and berries to string on my tree."

But instead of berries, Milly found a baby hedgehog, snoring softly in the snow.

"**Witchety whiskers!**" she gasped and tiptoed close. "He needs a better nest than that!"

So she wove all of her ivy into
a leafy blanket and gently tucked
it around him.

By the time Milly
had finished, the sky
was growing dark.
"**Fiddle!**" she fussed.
"It's too late to search
for berries now."
Milly scurried home.

There she found Felicity Finch and
her chicks, searching for food.
"What-oh-what shall we do?" the mother
bird cried. "The snow has covered our seeds."
"Come in where it's warm," said Milly.
"I've just made an apple-nut pie."

In the flick of a wing, the kitchen
was full of hungry chicks. Their feathers
fluttered and flapped as they flocked
around Milly's pie.

"Tasty-tasty!
Kind, how kind!"

they chirped.

And then they were gone—in a whoosh of feathers and dust. Milly sneezed.

Achoo! Achoo!

Nothing was left but scattered crumbs.

105

Milly heard a knock at the door. "**Fiddle!**" she muttered. "**What NOW?**"

"Berry Chribbas, Billy," called Gabriel Skunk.

"I brogg you a bresent. Berfume."

"**Perfume!**" said Milly, hiding a smile. "**Why, thank you.**"

Gabriel dabbed at his nose. "I hab a tebbible code."

"Try my hot honey punch," Milly said. "It's very good for a terrible cold."

Gabriel lifted the kettle and drank every drop.

"Thaggs," he said and ambled off home.

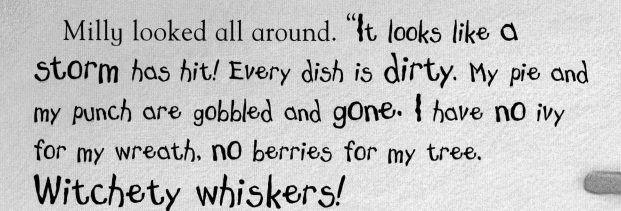

Milly looked all around. "It looks like a storm has hit! Every dish is dirty. My pie and my punch are gobbled and gone. I have no ivy for my wreath, no berries for my tree. Witchety whiskers!

Then Milly smiled. "At least I have my berfume...perfume from a skunk!" she giggled, and bustled off to bed. "The baby hedgehog is warm," she whispered. "The chicks are full of pie, and the punch will help dear Gabriel's cold." And with a yawn she fell asleep.

The next morning, Milly woke to a chorus of cheeps and chirps. Outside were robins, sparrows, and finches, and they were all singing—for her!

Behind the birds came a family of hedgehogs. Grandfather Hedgehog carried a sack, and the baby had flowers stuck in his prickly spines.

Cheepy-cheep!

Chirp!

Cheepy-cheep!

Last came Gabriel Skunk—with a
lopsided grin and a great big cake!
"**Goodness gracious!**" exclaimed
Milly. She invited them in.

They decorated the tree together with treasures from Grandfather Hedgehog's sack—buttons and ribbons, beads, paper clips, and all kinds of other odds and ends.

Milly's black eyes sparkled. "This is the very best Christmas ever! And I am the happiest mouse in the forest. Christmas just wouldn't be Christmas without my wonderful friends!"

MY FAVORITE CHRISTMAS STORIES

tiger tales
5 River Road, Suite 128, Wilton, CT 06897
Published in the United States 2015

ISBN-13: 978-1-68010-200-0
ISBN-10: 1-68010-200-1
Printed in China • LTP/1800/1188/0515

For more insight and activities,
visit us at www.tigertalesbooks.com

THE MAGICAL SNOWMAN

by Catherine Walters
Illustrated by Alison Edgson

First published in Great Britain 2009
by Little Tiger Press